Contents

The Inchcape Rock

By James Baldwin

In the North Sea there is a great rock called the Inchcape Rock. Many boats and ships have been wrecked on that rock, for it is so near the top of the water that no vessel can sail over it without striking it.

More than a hundred years ago there lived not far away a kind-hearted man who was called the Abbot of Aberbrothock. "It is a pity," he said, "that so many sailors should lose their lives on that rock."

So the abbot got a buoy fastened to the rock with a strong chain. It floated back and forth in the shallow water. On the top of the buoy was a bell, and when the waves dashed against it, the bell would ring out loud and clear.

Now, sailors were no longer afraid to cross the sea at that place. When they heard the bell ringing, they knew just where the rock was, and they steered their vessels around it. "God bless the good Abbot of Aberbrothock!" they all said.

One calm summer day, a ship with a black flag happened to sail not far from the Inchcape Rock. The ship belonged to a sea robber called Ralph the Rover. He was a terror to all honest people on sea and shore.

There was little wind that day, and the sea was as smooth as glass. The ship stood almost still – there was hardly a breath of air to fill her sails.

Ralph the Rover was walking on the

deck. He looked out upon the sea, and saw the buoy floating above the Inchcape Rock. But the bell was not ringing – there were no waves to set it in motion.

"Boys!" cried Ralph the Rover. "Put out the boat and row me to the Inchcape Rock. We will play a trick on the old abbot."

The boat was lowered. Strong arms soon rowed it to the Inchcape Rock. Then the robber, with a heavy ax, broke the chain that held the buoy. He cut the fastenings of the bell and it fell into the water. There was a gurgling sound as it sank out of sight.

"The next one that comes this way will not bless the abbot," said Ralph the Rover.

Soon a breeze sprang up and the black ship sailed away. The sea robber laughed as he looked back and saw that there was nothing to mark the place of the rock.

For many days, Ralph the Rover scoured the seas, and plundered many ships. At last he chanced to sail back toward the place from which he had started.

The wind had blown hard all day. The waves rolled high. The ship was moving swiftly. But in the evening the wind died away, and a thick fog came on.

Ralph the Rover walked the deck. He could not see where the ship was going. "If the fog would only clear away!" he said.

"I thought I heard the roar of breakers," said the pilot. "We must be near the shore."

"I cannot tell," said Ralph the Rover, "but I think we are not far from the

Inchcape Rock. I wish we could hear the good abbot's bell."

The next moment there was a great crash. "It is the Inchcape Rock!" the sailors cried, as the ship gave a lurch to one side, and began to sink.

"Oh, what a wretch am I!" cried Ralph the Rover. "This is what comes of the joke that I played on the good abbot!"

What was it that he heard as the waves rushed over him? Was it the abbot's bell, ringing for him far down at the bottom of the sea?

The Cat and the Mouse

By Joseph Jacobs

The cat and the mouse played together in the malthouse.

The cat bit the mouse's tail off. "Pray, puss, give me my tail," begged the mouse.

"No," said the cat, "I'll not give you your tail, till you go to the cow and fetch me some milk."

First the mouse leaped and then she ran, till she came to the cow, and thus began:

"Pray, cow, give me milk, that I may give cat milk, that cat may give me my own tail again."

"No," said the cow, "I will give you no milk, till you go to the farmer and get me some hay."

First the mouse leaped, and then she ran, till she came to the farmer and thus began:

"Pray, farmer, give me hay, that I may give cow hay, that cow may give me milk, that I may give cat milk, that cat may give me my own tail again."

"No," said the farmer, "I'll give you no hay, till you go to the butcher and fetch me some meat."

First the mouse leaped, and then she ran, till she came to the butcher, and thus began:

"Pray, butcher, give me meat, that I may give farmer meat, that farmer may give me hay, that I may give cow hay, that cow may give me milk, that I may give cat milk, that cat may give me my own tail again."

"No," said the butcher, "I'll give you no meat, till you go to the baker and fetch me some bread."

First the mouse leapt and then she ran, till she came to the baker, and thus began:

"Pray, baker, give me bread, that I may give butcher bread, that butcher may give me meat, that I may give farmer meat, that farmer may give me hay, that I may give cow hay, that cow may give me milk, that I

may give cat milk,
that cat may give me my
own tail again."

"Yes," said the baker, "I'll give you some bread, but if you eat my meal, I'll cut off your head."

Then the baker gave mouse bread, and mouse gave butcher bread, and butcher gave mouse meat, and mouse gave farmer meat, and farmer

gave mouse hay, and mouse gave cow hay, and cow gave mouse milk, and mouse gave cat milk, and cat gave mouse her own tail again!

The Open Road

An extract from *The Wind in the Willows*
by Kenneth Grahame

The Mole has just moved into a new home at the riverbank when he makes friends with the Water Rat, who introduces him to the joy of messing around in boats…

"Ratty," said Mole, "what I wanted to ask you was, won't you take me to call on Mr. Toad? I've heard so much about him, and I would like to make his acquaintance."

"Why, certainly," said the good-natured

Rat, jumping to his feet. "Get the boat out, and we'll paddle up there at once. It's never the wrong time to call on Toad. Early or late, he's always the same fellow. Always good-tempered, always glad to see you, always sorry when you go!"

"He must be a very nice animal," observed the Mole, as he got into the boat and took the sculls, while the Rat settled himself comfortably in the stern.

"He is indeed the best of animals," replied Rat. "So simple, so good-natured, and so affectionate. Perhaps he's not very clever – we can't all be geniuses – and it may be that he is both boastful and conceited. But he has got some great qualities, has Toady."

Rounding a bend in the river, they came in sight of a handsome, dignified old house of mellowed red brick, with well-kept lawns reaching down to the water's edge.

"There's Toad Hall," said the Rat.

They glided up the creek, and the Mole slipped his sculls as they passed into the shadow of a large boathouse. Here they saw many handsome boats, but none in the water. The place had an unused air.

The Rat looked around him. "I understand," said he. "Boating is played out. He's tired of it and done with it. I wonder what new fad he has taken up now?"

They disembarked and strolled across the flower-decked lawns in search of Toad, whom they presently happened upon in a wicker garden chair, with a preoccupied expression on his face, and a large map spread out on his knees.

"Hooray!" he cried, jumping up on seeing them. "This is splendid!" He shook the paws of both of them warmly, never waiting for an introduction to the Mole. "I need both of you – badly! You've got to help me. It's most important!"

"It's about your rowing, I suppose," said the Rat. "You're getting on fairly well, though you splash a good bit still. With a great deal of patience, and any quantity of coaching, you may—"

"Oh, pooh! Boating!" interrupted the Toad, in great disgust. "Silly boyish amusement. I've given that up. Waste of time, that's what it is. No, I've discovered the real thing. Come with me, and you shall see what you shall see!"

He led the way to the stable yard, the Rat following with a most mistrustful expression. There, drawn out of the coach house, they saw a gypsy caravan, shining with newness, painted a canary-yellow picked out with green, and red wheels.

"There you are!" cried the Toad, puffing out his chest with pride. "There's real life for you, embodied in that little cart. The open road, the dusty highway, the heath, the common, the rolling hills! Camps, villages, towns, cities! Here today, up and off to somewhere else tomorrow! Travel, change, interest, excitement! The world before you, and a horizon that's always changing! And mind – this is the very finest cart of its sort, without any exception! Come inside and look at the arrangements. Planned 'em all myself, I did!"

The Mole was tremendously interested and excited, and

followed the Toad eagerly up the steps and inside. The Rat only snorted and thrust his hands deep into his pockets, remaining where he was.

It was indeed very compact and comfortable. Little sleeping bunks, a little table that folded up against the wall, a cooking stove, lockers, bookshelves, a birdcage with a bird in it, and pots, pans, jugs and kettles of every size and variety.

"All complete!" said the Toad triumphantly, pulling open a locker. "You see – cookies, potted lobster, sardines – everything you can possibly want. Soda water here, letter paper, bacon, jelly, cards and dominoes there. You'll find," he continued, as they descended the steps again, "that nothing has been forgotten, when we make our start this afternoon."

"I beg your pardon," said the Rat slowly, as he chewed a straw, "but did I overhear you say something about 'we', and 'start', and 'this afternoon'?"

"Now, you dear good old Ratty," said Toad, imploringly, "don't begin talking in that sniffy sort of way, because you know you really have *got* to come. I can't possibly manage without you, so please consider it settled, and don't argue – it's the one thing I can't stand. You surely don't mean to stick to your dull, stinky old river all your life, and just live in a hole in a bank, and *boat*? I want to show you the world, Ratty! I'm going to make an *animal* of you, my boy!"

"I don't care," said the Rat, doggedly. "I'm not coming, and that's flat. And I *am* going to stick to my old river, *and* live in a hole, *and* boat, as I've always done. And what's more, Mole's going to stick with me and do as I do, aren't you, Mole?"

"Of course I am," said the Mole, loyally. "I'll always stick to you, Rat, and what you say is to be – has got to be. All the same, it sounds as if it might have been – well, rather fun, you know!" he added, wistfully. Poor Mole! The Life Adventurous was so new a thing to him and so thrilling, and this fresh aspect of it was so tempting, and he had fallen in love at first sight with the canary-colored cart.

The Rat saw what was passing in his

mind, and wavered. He hated disappointing people, and he was awfully fond of the Mole, and would do almost anything to oblige him. Toad was watching both of them closely.

"Come along in and have some lunch," he said, "and we'll talk it over. We needn't decide anything in a hurry. Of course, I don't really care. I only want to give pleasure to you fellows. 'Live for others!' That's my motto in life."

Needless to say, after lunch, the old gray horse was caught and harnessed. Toad packed the lockers with necessaries, and hung nosebags, onions, bundles of hay, and baskets from the bottom of the cart.

They set off, all talking at once, each

The Open Road

animal either trudging by the side of the cart or sitting on the shaft. It was a golden afternoon. The smell of the dust they kicked up was rich and satisfying. Out of orchards on either side of the road, birds called and whistled to them cheerily. Good-natured wayfarers called, "Good-day," or stopped to say nice things about their cart. Rabbits, sitting at their front doors held up their forepaws and exclaimed, "Oh my! Oh my! Oh my!"

They had a pleasant ramble over grassy downs and along narrow by-lanes, until at last they came out on the high road – and there disaster sprang out on them.

Far behind them they heard a faint warning hum, like the drone of a distant bee. Glancing back, they saw a small cloud of dust, with a dark center of energy, advancing on them at incredible speed, while from out of the dust a faint 'Poop-poop!' wailed like an uneasy animal. Hardly regarding it, they turned to resume their conversation, when in an instant (as it seemed) the peaceful scene was changed, with a blast of wind and a whirl of sound that made them jump for the nearest ditch.

It was on them! The 'Poop-poop' rang with a brazen shout in their ears. They had a moment's glimpse of an interior of glittering plate-glass and rich leather. The magnificent motor car with its pilot tense and hugging his wheel, possessed all earth and air for the fraction of a second. Then up flew an enveloping cloud of dust that enwrapped them, and the car dwindled to a speck in the far distance, changed back into a droning bee once more.

The old gray horse, dreaming, as he plodded along, of his quiet paddock, in a new raw situation such as this abandoned himself to his natural emotions. Rearing, plunging, backing steadily, he drove the cart backward toward the ditch at the side of the road. It wavered an instant – then there was a heart-rending *crash* – and the canary-colored cart, their pride and joy, lay on its side in the ditch, an irredeemable wreck.

The Rat danced up and down in the road, simply transported with passion. "You villains!" he shouted after it, shaking both fists, "You scoundrels, you highwaymen, you – you – roadhogs! I'll have the law on you! I'll report you! I'll take you through all the courts!"

Meanwhile, Toad sat straight down in the middle of the dusty road, his legs stretched out before him, and stared fixedly in the direction of the disappearing motor car. He breathed short, his face wore a placid satisfied expression, and at intervals he murmured, "Poop-poop!"

The Mole was busy trying to calm the horse, which he succeeded in doing after a time. Then he went to look at the cart on its side in the ditch. It was indeed a sorry sight. Panels and windows smashed, axles hopelessly bent, one wheel off, sardine tins scattered over the wide world, and the bird in the birdcage sobbing pitifully and calling to be let out.

The Rat came to help him, but their united efforts were not sufficient to right the cart. "Hi! Toad!" they cried. "Come and lend a hand, will you!"

The Toad never answered a word, or

budged from his seat in the road, so they went to see what was the matter with him. They found him in a sort of a trance, a happy smile on his face, his eyes still fixed on the dusty wake of their destroyer. At intervals he was still heard to murmur, "Poop-poop!"

The Rat shook him by the shoulder. "Are you coming to help us, Toad?" he demanded sternly.

"Glorious, stirring sight!" murmured Toad, never offering to move. "The poetry of motion! The *real* way to travel! The *only* way to travel! Here today – in next week tomorrow! Villages skipped, towns and cities jumped – always somebody else's horizon! Oh bliss! Oh poop-poop! Oh my! Oh my!"

"Oh *stop*!" cried the Mole despairingly.

"And to think I never *knew*!" went on the Toad in a dreamy monotone. "All those wasted years that lie behind me, I never knew, never even *dreamed*! But *now* – but now that I know, now that I fully realize! Oh what a flowery track lies spread before me, henceforth! What dust clouds shall spring up behind me as I speed on my reckless way! What carts I shall fling carelessly into the ditch in the wake of my magnificent onset! Horrid little carts – common carts – canary-colored carts!"

"What are we to do with him?" asked the Mole of the Water Rat.

"Nothing at all," replied the Rat firmly. "Because there is really nothing to be done.

You see, I know him from of old. He is now possessed. He has got a new craze, and it always takes him that way in its first stage. He'll continue like that for days now. Never mind him. Let's go and see what there is to be done about the cart."

A careful inspection showed them that, even if they succeeded in righting it by themselves, the cart would travel no longer. The axles were in a hopeless state, and the missing wheel was shattered into pieces.

The Rat knotted the horse's reins over his back and took him by the head, carrying the birdcage and its hysterical occupant in his other hand. "Come on!" he said grimly to the Mole. "It's five or six miles to the nearest town, and we shall just have to walk

it. The sooner we make a start the better."

"But what about Toad?" asked the Mole anxiously. "We can't leave him here, in the state he's in! It's not safe. Supposing another Thing were to come along?"

"Oh, *bother* Toad," said the Rat savagely, "I've done with him!"

They had not proceeded far when there was a pattering behind them. Toad caught them up and thrust a paw inside the elbow of each of them, still breathing short and staring into vacancy.

"Now, look here, Toad!" said the Rat. "As

soon as we get to the town, you'll have to go straight to the police station, see if they know anything about that motor car, and lodge a complaint. Then you'll have to arrange for the cart to be fetched and mended. Meanwhile the Mole and I will find an inn where we can stay till the cart's ready."

"Police station!" murmured Toad dreamily. "Me *complain* of that vision! *Mend the cart!* I never want to see that cart again. Oh, Ratty! You can't think how obliged I am to you for coming on this trip! I wouldn't have gone without you, then I might never have seen that swan, that sunbeam! I owe it all to you, my friends!"

The Rat turned from him in despair.

"He's hopeless" he said to the Mole. "When we get to the town we'll go to the railway station. We may pick up a train that'll get us back to the riverbank. *Never* let me go looking for fun with this animal again!"

The following evening Mole was fishing on the bank, when the Rat came along. "Heard the news?" he said. "Toad went to town this morning. He has ordered a large and very expensive motor car."

Why the Bear is Stumpy-Tailed

By Sir George Webbe Dasent

One wintry day, when the fields were covered with snow and ice, and none of the animals could find food, Bruin the Bear met Reynard the Fox. To his surprise, Reynard was slinking along with a string of fish. How Bruin's stomach rumbled! Little did he know that Reynard had stolen them from the home of a farmer down the road. The slow old bear thought that the cunning fox

must have come by them himself.

"Where ever did you find those?" asked the Bear, licking his lips.

"Oh my Lord Bruin, I've been out fishing and caught them," said Reynard the Fox.

So Bruin had a mind to learn to fish too. He begged Reynard to tell him where to go and how to set about it.

"Oh, it will be an easy craft for you," answered the Fox. "All you've got to do is go out on the lake over the ice, cut a hole and stick your tail down into it. Then go on holding it there as long as you can. Take no notice if your tail smarts a little – that's when the fish bite. Then, when you can wait no longer, pull your tail out as fast and as hard as you can."

Yes, Bruin the Bear did as Reynard the Fox had said, and held his tail a long, long time down in the hole, till it was fast frozen in. Then he pulled it out with a speedy, strong pull – and it snapped short off!

And that's why bears go about with a stumpy tail this very day.